Erick,

Thanks for your support!

MW00764266

THE
JELLYFISH MONSTER

by Bryan Kwasnik
Illustrated by Jackie Hahn

Mascot Books
560 Herndon Parkway #120
Herndon, VA 20170

info@mascotbooks.com
PROPM1115A
Library of Congress Control Number: 2015915677

ISBN-13: 978-1-63177-182-8

Printed in the United States

www.mascotbooks.com

Dedicated to my family and all the summer
vacations we shared together.

CHAPTER 1

Billy sat in the shallow water as the waves rushed past him and then crawled back to sea. The water was only about ankle deep, but Billy was content with just digging into the dark, wet sand in front of him, looking out towards the horizon. His two brothers, Sam and Jeremy, were sitting on top of inner tubes hitting each other with foam noodles as the waves tossed them around. His parents had gone for a walk down the shoreline to look at the new condos that were under construction. They asked if he wanted to come with them, but Billy shook his head no. Billy just kept clutching the clay-like sand in his fists, lifting it out of the water, and dumping it behind him.

The sky was cloudless and the hot sun poured down on Billy's sun block covered face. Even though it was so hot, the water underneath Billy was cold and there was a nice breeze coming off the ocean so he was comfortable.

The hole he was making was very quickly filled

in by waves and the sand around it was falling into the opening. However, he was still making noticeable progress. He found a couple of white scallop shells, a broken orange spiral looking shell, a few rocks, and a crushed Pepsi can.

Billy watched boogie boarders narrowly avoid collision with each other and other swimmers. While he watched one man tip over as a wave crashed on top of him, Billy touched something sharp. He reached into the sand where he was digging and found a long, spiral shell with its tip sticking up towards the sky. He couldn't tell how big it was because only the very top was visible. He tried pulling it but it wouldn't budge so he dug some more, quickly trying to fight the waves as they deposited more and more sand to impede his progress.

After about ten minutes, and with more of the shell in sight, Billy tried again to the remove the spiral from the sand. Still nothing. *It must be huge!* he thought to himself. He renewed his digging with even more vigor and after another ten minutes or so he stood up, bent down, grabbed the

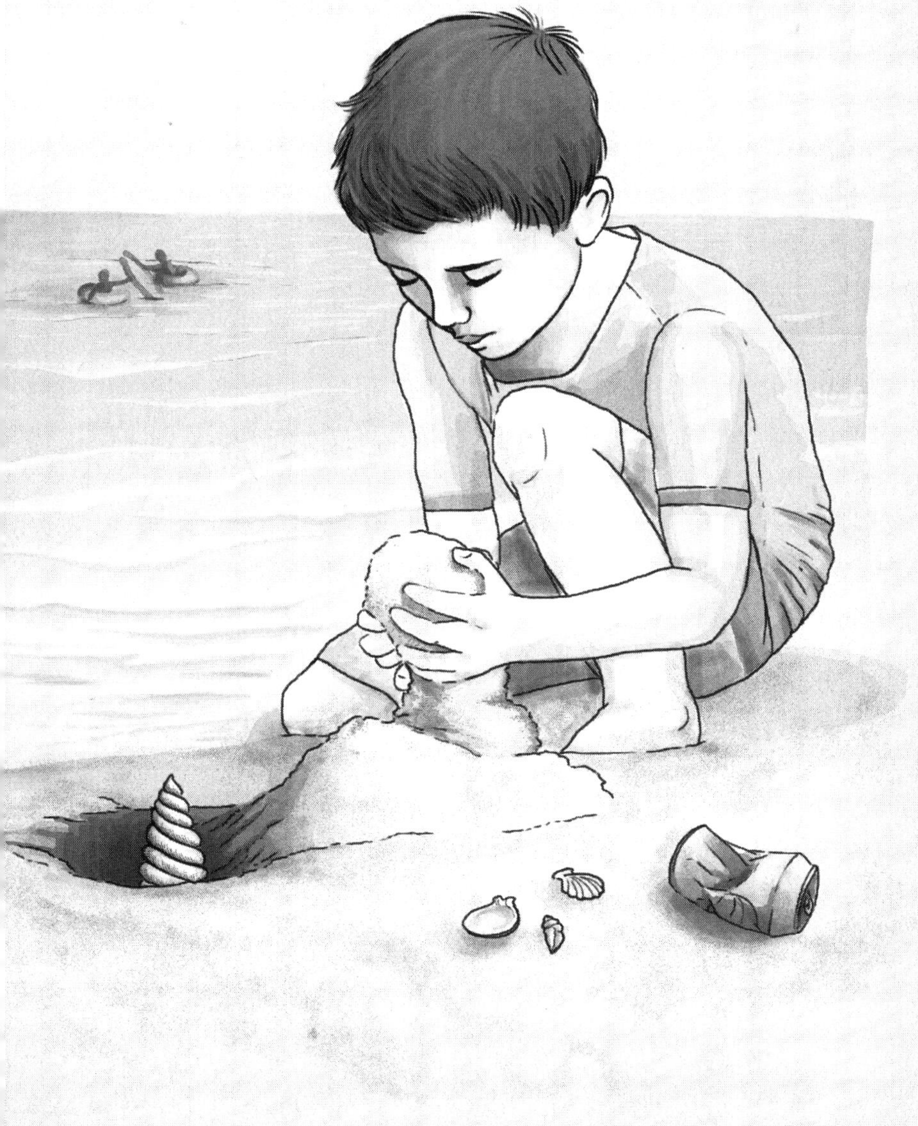

shell and pulled with all his strength. At first it didn't seem to be working but then something came loose from the sand and Billy fell backwards from the force, landing with a splash.

Standing in front of him was the strangest thing he had ever seen. The spiral shell was actually a horn attached to a round jellyfish head with big black eyes and translucent skin that allowed the bright sunlight behind it to pass through. Its thin and curly tentacles hung around the bottom of his head like a beard covering his dark green shoulders. Seaweed was draped over its shoulders and clung to its body like clothing. Its hands and feet were webbed and it had large, spiky fins along its spine.

CHAPTER 2

Billy stood open mouthed. The Jellyfish Monster stared blankly at him. Billy thought about screaming, but somehow the creature seemed harmless. The monster blinked its large, black eyes, raised a hand, and waved it back and forth. Billy waved back, not knowing what else to do. Then the Jellyfish Monster's tentacles rose up and fell back down like they were waving as well and a large bubble appeared around Billy and the creature. The bubble shook and they sank into the sand.

Billy watched as the world disappeared while no one around him seemed to notice he was sinking into the sand in a giant bubble. They started tunneling past shells, and tiny clams, and hermit crabs whose little mouths moved and released small bubbles as if a word was trapped in each one.

They moved faster and faster and Billy felt like he was on a roller coaster. They passed by fish skeletons and dinosaur bones as well as stranger things that Billy would need a trip to the library to identify. Finally, they started to rise. When they did they were at the bottom of the ocean. Above, the sunlight looked so far away.

"Are you going to eat me now?" Billy asked.

The Jellyfish Monster didn't answer; it just turned to the left and looked out into the dark ocean. Billy turned the same way but couldn't see anything at first. A large shadow approached that seemed to stretch across the entire sea. It was dark blue and massive. It swayed up and down as it floated gracefully towards them with its two flippers and long tail, the tip of which Billy could see when it was all the way up or down.

As it came closer, Billy could see a large eye staring out from the enormous whale. It opened its huge mouth filled with large bristly teeth and the bubble carrying Billy and the Jellyfish Monster was swept inside.

It was dark and the bubble rocked back and forth on the whale's bumpy tongue. Moving towards them out of the darkness was a metal bucket wedged into a lifesaver with the word "Titanic" written on it in bold, blocky letters. It was pulled

towards Billy and the Jellyfish Monster by a small salamander-like creature. It had tiny legs that were paddling frantically as it dragged the lifesaver with its tail.

The salamander was orange with blue swirls that glowed in the dark. Its eyes were bright blue as well. It was covered with tiny frills that swayed as it moved. As it approached, Billy noticed its skin was see-through and he could see the salamander's tiny heart pumping quickly.

The Jellyfish Monster reached its arm out of

the bubble and dropped a sand dollar into the bucket floating in the lifesaver. The salamander then turned and swam away from them.

Billy listened to strange, echo-y noises and numerous whale calls that were muffled by the layers of bubble and blubber between him and the outside world. Billy pinched his arm to make sure he wasn't dreaming. It hurt, so he couldn't be asleep. At least that's what everyone says.

After awhile Billy's eyes adjusted to the darkness. The Jellyfish Monster was standing still, moving gently with the motion of the whale they were riding.

"Are we really inside an animal?" Billy asked him, still not one hundred percent convinced.

Just then the giant creature burped. It was louder than the Fourth of July fireworks Billy's town always set off. And it stunk.

Billy grabbed his nose with both hands to keep the smell out. He looked up and saw that the Jellyfish Monster was doing the same thing, even though it didn't look like it even had a nose.

"How much longer is this going to take?" Billy

asked with his nose still covered.

The Jellyfish Monster shrugged.

CHAPTER 3

At one point the creature carrying Billy and the Jellyfish Monster slowed down and opened its mouth. A large octopus swam in. It was almost twice the size of the Jellyfish Monster with dark red skin and orange spots. All but one of its eight arms was carrying something.

In one was a basket full of colorful sea plants. In another was a shovel. The rest of the arms held

other tools, but in one was a small glass box, like a fish tank. Inside was a small, brown bunny rabbit. It sat calmly, wiggling its nose and chewing on a piece of straw.

Billy waved at the octopus and it waved back politely with its free arm. The Jellyfish Monster waved as well.

After a few minutes the creature opened its mouth again and a school of yellow fish swam in along with a family of sea turtles. The yellow fish would not stay still and swam around all over the

place. One bumped into the bubble Billy was in. It blushed and then darted away, embarrassed.

"Is this like a bus?" he asked the Jellyfish Monster, but it didn't look like it knew what a bus was.

A walrus got in a few minutes later. Its plump body moved slowly to a clear space away from the other passengers. The walrus then took out a newspaper and began to read it. Its dark whiskers twitched as it scanned the pages.

At the next stop a Merman came aboard. He had the body of a man, but with a big, green, scaly fish head.

"I guess the movies got it wrong," Billy said to the Merman. The Merman tilted his head to the side in confusion and then looked away. His mouth hung open as he stood there, staring into space.

Again, a couple minutes later, another crowd of passengers got in. Eels, shrimp, sea horses, and there was even a killer whale!

The salamander navigated his way through the thick group pausing to accept a sand dollar from each one. The lifesaver often got stuck and the salamander spent more time struggling with it than requesting payment.

The orca squeezed its way into the group and when it finally settled it was against the bubble, pushing it in almost to Billy's face. Billy was afraid the bubble was going to pop and he would drown.

It was a good thing that many of the passengers got out a few minutes later. Billy relaxed a bit once they left and the bubble went back to its original shape and size.

After a time, Billy and the Jellyfish Monster were the only ones left. Without warning, the giant whale opened its mouth and spit out the bubble.

The bubble spun around wildly as it exited the creature and Billy got so dizzy he thought he was going to be sick. Luckily, the bubble slowed and stopped spinning and Billy avoided losing his breakfast. He looked around to see where they were and saw that they were floating above a large, colorful city.

CHAPTER 4

There were shells and coral as big as skyscrapers each with "windows" that had lights shining out of them. The coral buildings were arranged in every shape. Some were simple, while others had grown in every direction creating amazing architecture that designers could only dream of.

There were large mountains of rock littered with caves. There was a step pyramid made out of turtle shells. A barnacle-covered submarine stood vertically, another tower in the skyline.

Colorful plants grew on all of the structures decorating the city. There was movement everywhere, as fish and sea creatures jostled around the busy metropolis.

They sank down to an opening in the city filled with tree-like purple and orange sea anemones swaying from side to side. The anemones were arranged in rows like a park with shell-lined paths between them.

Billy drifted along one of the paths passing two

crabs as big as he was. They were holding hands (or claws rather). There was a lobster walking a sea slug and a school of black and white fish darting in between the "trees".

Floating along the paths were light bulb shaped jellyfish that glowed pink and acted like streetlights. At one point there was a crowd of fish watching a purple octopus make paintings in the water using its own ink. It was currently sketching what looked to be a school of dolphins jumping out of a large wave. Behind the octopus, its previous paintings of a seagull and a field of sea flowers hung suspended in the water.

They left the path and came to a large, open field of sea grass. There was a stage made out of two sunken airplanes that looked like they were from the 1940s. On the connected wings were several other boys and girls inside bubbles. They were all standing next to other Jellyfish Monsters; some were taller than the one with Billy, and others were short and round.

Some had blue bodies and some had red. There was even a white one with black and brown spots. Their heads were all translucent and they all had the same big, black eyes. Their tentacles were different shades of pink and purple and blue. There were seven in all, and Billy and his strange companion made eight.

Surrounding the stage was a crowd comprised of fish and crustaceans and a few octopi. Some were holding bubbles attached to seaweed like balloons. On the right side below the stage were eight sharks tied to a huge anchor. But these sharks didn't look anything like normal sharks.

The first was a bull shark. The only reason Billy could tell was because its head was actually shaped like a bull; a flat nose stood at the end of its head with a ring through it and it had two black horns on top of its head.

The next was orange with black stripes and had the face of a tiger complete with yellow fangs and pointed ears.

The third was an angel shark that had wings instead of fins. A white leopard shark with black spots was growling beside it.

There was a goblin shark that just looked like a goblin shark which was already strange enough (Billy had seen them on *Shark Week* one year).

Next to it was a hammerhead shark that was constantly changing colors and blending in with the scenery around it (like a chameleon), and a ghost shark that had translucent, white skin that showed all the shark's insides. At times it seemed to vanish entirely.

The last shark was white and had black stripes. It had a thin mane of black hair on its head swaying in the ocean currents. *A zebra shark*, Billy thought.

Billy was directed to the zebra shark and as he approached the bubble around him shrank until it was just around his head like a helmet. His body felt cold when it was suddenly exposed to the water, but he quickly got used to it. He took a seat on top of the zebra shark and held onto its mane.

There was a girl next to him in a purple bathing suit. She had brown skin and black hair tied up in a bun.

"Hi," he said. His words sounded all warbled travelling through the bubble and the water.

"Hello, I'm Michelle," she said cheerfully.

"I'm Billy," he responded. "Do you know where

we are?"

She shook her head. "No, I was in Florida with my family making a sandcastle on the beach and then suddenly this big monster thing brought me under the sea."

"Wow, you're all the way from Florida? I was at Wildwood in New Jersey."

"Really? This is so weird." She looked down and gasped as the ghost shark disappeared for a moment. "Is this even real?"

"I think so."

The Jellyfish Monster swam over to Billy and patted him on the head. Bubbles came out from under his tentacles where his mouth was hidden but Billy couldn't understand what it was saying.

"I think we're supposed to race," Michelle said.

"Race?"

"Yeah, we're all lined up on these shark things."

Billy looked down the line at the other kids and their sharks. The sharks growled and snapped their teeth impatiently. They knew what was about to happen. Billy hoped it didn't involve getting eaten.

CHAPTER 5

A creature with a large puffer fish head and tiny human-like body covered in golden scales swam on stage. It was wearing a bow tie made out of seaweed. It addressed the crowd in a high-pitched whistle that Billy couldn't understand. The creature's large head filled up like a balloon before each thing it said and shrank back down by the end of the phrase.

The puffer fish spoke for some time. The fish in the crowd seemed like they were yawning, and one old lobster appeared to have fallen asleep.

Finally, the puffer fish ended his speech and motioned towards the eight children on their sharks. The crowd cheered. A big crab side stepped over to them and placed its claw around the ropes holding the sharks to the anchor. The crowd started making noise in unison and Billy could tell it was a countdown.

Suddenly the rope was cut and the sharks sped forward. A cloud of sand was kicked up and

momentarily obscured Billy's vision. As it cleared, he watched Michelle disappear around a bend. All the sharks were gone except Billy - Billy wasn't moving at all. He looked down at his zebra shark and tried kicking his heels and pulling on its mane. It wouldn't budge. "Come on," he pleaded. The shark simply started calmly grazing on the sea grass.

Billy looked over and saw the Jellyfish Monster had his hands on his head and was shaking it back and forth. "I don't know what to do," Billy explained but no one could understand him. It looked like many fish were laughing at him. "Come on! The race started, we have to move!" he shouted at the shark. It gave no indication that it heard him.

How many seconds had passed? Billy couldn't tell. He figured he would have no chance of winning now because everyone else had such a head start. He considered giving up and swimming away from the shark, but decided he wanted to try, even if he wouldn't win. Billy continued kicking his legs and patting the shark trying to coax it to move.

Finally Billy pulled on the shark's ears to get its attention and then pointed towards where the rest went. He kicked his heels once more and yelled "giddy-up!" and the zebra shark started with a jolt and raced around the bend.

Billy held on tight for fear of falling off. The shark weaved through the rows of algae, kelp, and yellow sun coral and Billy could just make out the other sharks in the distance. The path he was on opened up and they approached a giant cliff. Billy felt like he was about to plummet even though he was underwater. As they passed over the cliff Billy saw that another boy who was riding the goblin shark had stopped right before the cliff, apparently too frightened to continue. *One down*, he thought to himself.

Billy's shark went over the cliff and started swimming down deeper into the water. The shark spun gleefully as it swam. Billy hadn't expected that, and almost fell off. He held on tighter.

There was a narrow ravine near the bottom, possibly a trench of some kind. Billy had learned about them in school. Tiny fish flew past as they gained speed, diving faster and faster. Billy's hands hurt from holding on so tight. It was dark in the trench and the light above seemed so far away and disappeared the farther they traveled. Billy lost sight of all the other racers and the darkness swallowed the light completely.

CHAPTER 6

Looking ahead through the dark water, Billy could see some blinking lights. There were flashes of blues and green and reds. *What is that?* he thought to himself. As his shark approached, the lights grew brighter and multiplied. They reminded Billy of stars in the night sky. He gasped when he finally realized what they were – thousands of bioluminescent jellyfish, squid, and fish.

The bottom was covered in glowing creatures even stranger than the ones he had already seen. They were strange shapes and some were completely see-through. Many reminded him of horror movie posters, with needle-like teeth and big, scary eyes. Some didn't even look like animals at all. Neon lights flickered in hundreds of patterns and colors, no two were exactly alike. It was hypnotizing.

The shark pulled up and leveled out as they reached the squirming, glowing floor of the trench. Their path was now lit and Billy could see the other children in front of them traveling above

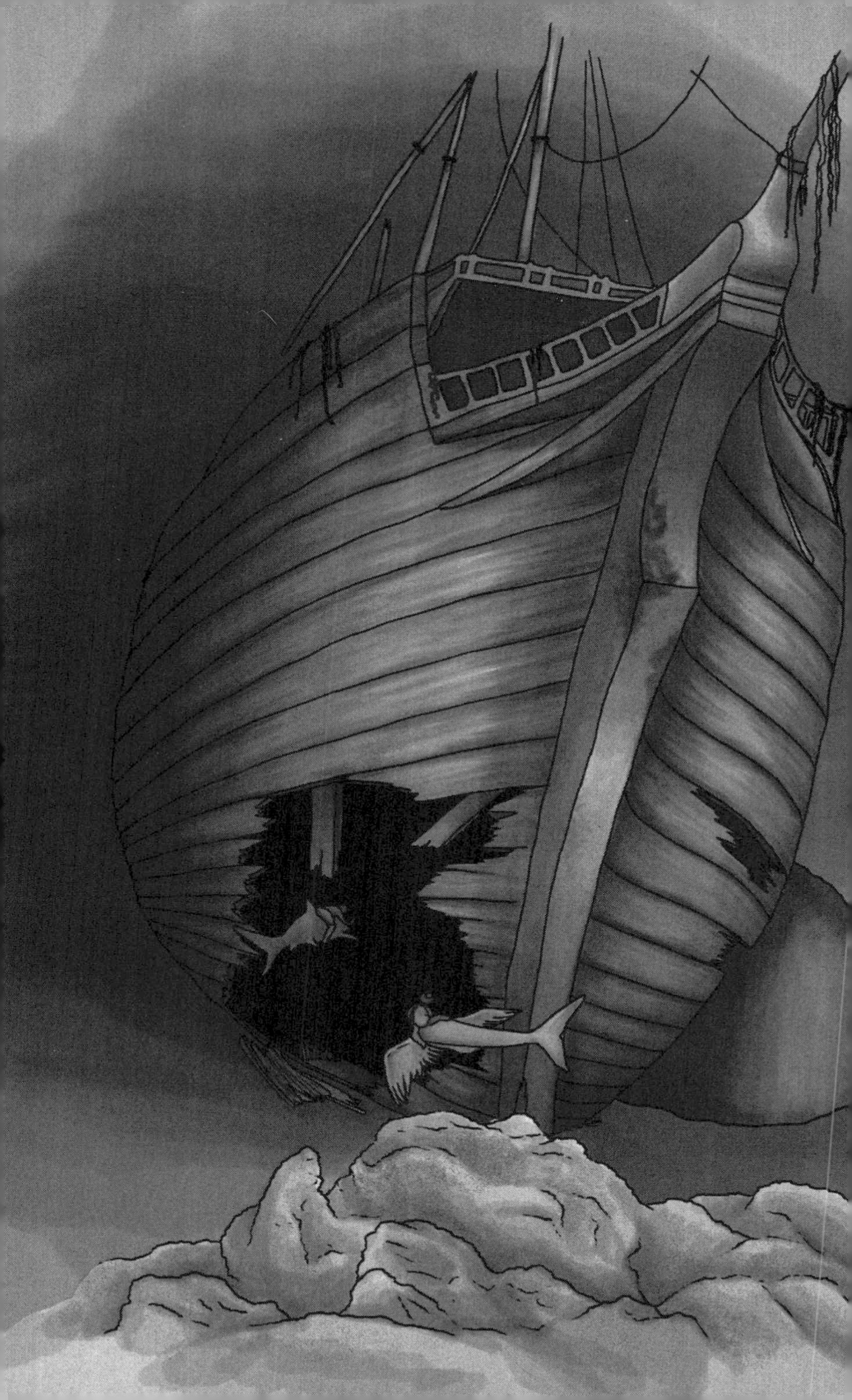

the curious animals and crustaceans blinking an unheard language. The closest appeared to be the white leopard shark whose skin seemed to change color each time the lights flashed from below and reflected off its scales.

Billy and his shark made a sharp right as the trench began to zigzag. They twisted left and right and left and right at each turn. Billy's legs were extended behind him as he held on to the saddle for dear life. He was getting dizzy from all the motion, but luckily the path straightened out.

They were getting closer to the leopard shark and Billy kicked his heels to make the zebra shark swim faster. Before long they were neck and neck. He turned to look at the girl riding the shark. She was wearing a red bathing suit and had a very determined look on her face.

Suddenly, the trench began to narrow into a cave and Billy could see there would be room for only one shark to pass at a time. "Come on!" he yelled to the shark to encourage it to finally pass their opponent just in the nick of time.

The stone walls of the trench were inches away

on either side of him. It was pitch black again, all the glowing creatures were behind them and the sun was miles above. He held on anxiously and wondered if it was possible to sweat underwater.

The path began to ascend and they traveled up and up. Billy could see light ahead of them. The light grew brighter, and Billy squinted as they finally burst out into a forest of seaweed.

The sun was above them causing the sand below to sparkle. The leaves of seaweed lashed at Billy's face and he swung his hands around to keep them away. He could see the plants rustling ahead of him and judged that there were two other racers about a basketball court away.

The seaweed ended and Billy gasped. A giant pirate ship loomed menacingly in front of them. It was slightly slanted, resting against a large rock. The ship was enormous and had a large hole in the bottom of it. One of its large masts had snapped in half and fallen onto the deck of the ship.

Billy could see the two racers in front of him enter the ship through the opening; it was the bull shark and the angel shark.

CHAPTER 7

They entered the wooden wreck and immediately turned left. They rushed through several small rooms filled with old wooden barrels, nets, cannonballs, and skeletons. Billy tried to imagine the exciting adventures and terrifying battles the vessel had encountered. They reached the end of the ship and turned quickly to swim up the stairs to the next level.

As they entered a large room lined with cannons on either side, Billy could see one of the sharks at the end of the room. It was the bull shark and it had gotten its horns stuck in the wooden beams of the walls. It tried to wrestle itself free, but it didn't look like it was working. When Billy and his shark left the room he turned and saw that the horns had gone all the way through the wall and one horn was stuck in the side of a large crate.

Billy swam through another room filled with guns and swords and other old weapons that were rusted and growing barnacles. They had reached the other end of the ship and turned up another set of stairs. They were in a medium sized room that had a round table in the center.

Six skeletons were sitting around it wearing pirate clothes (some with eye patches or a hook hand). The table was covered with gold and sparkling jewels. One boy was currently busy scooping up as much as he could; he had leaped off the angel shark to grab the treasure. The shark was in the corner of the room pacing impatiently.

As they left the treasure room they were on the main deck of the ship with two masts towering above them displaying tattered sails. As the zebra shark swam through a large tear in the largest sail, Billy did a quick count in his head. There were three more racers in front of him. *We might win!* he thought excitedly.

They swam away from the pirate ship and towards a large, tangled cluster of red coral that went on for miles in either direction. Billy saw the tiger shark enter it ahead of them. He kicked his heels and headed into the maze of coral and sea anemones.

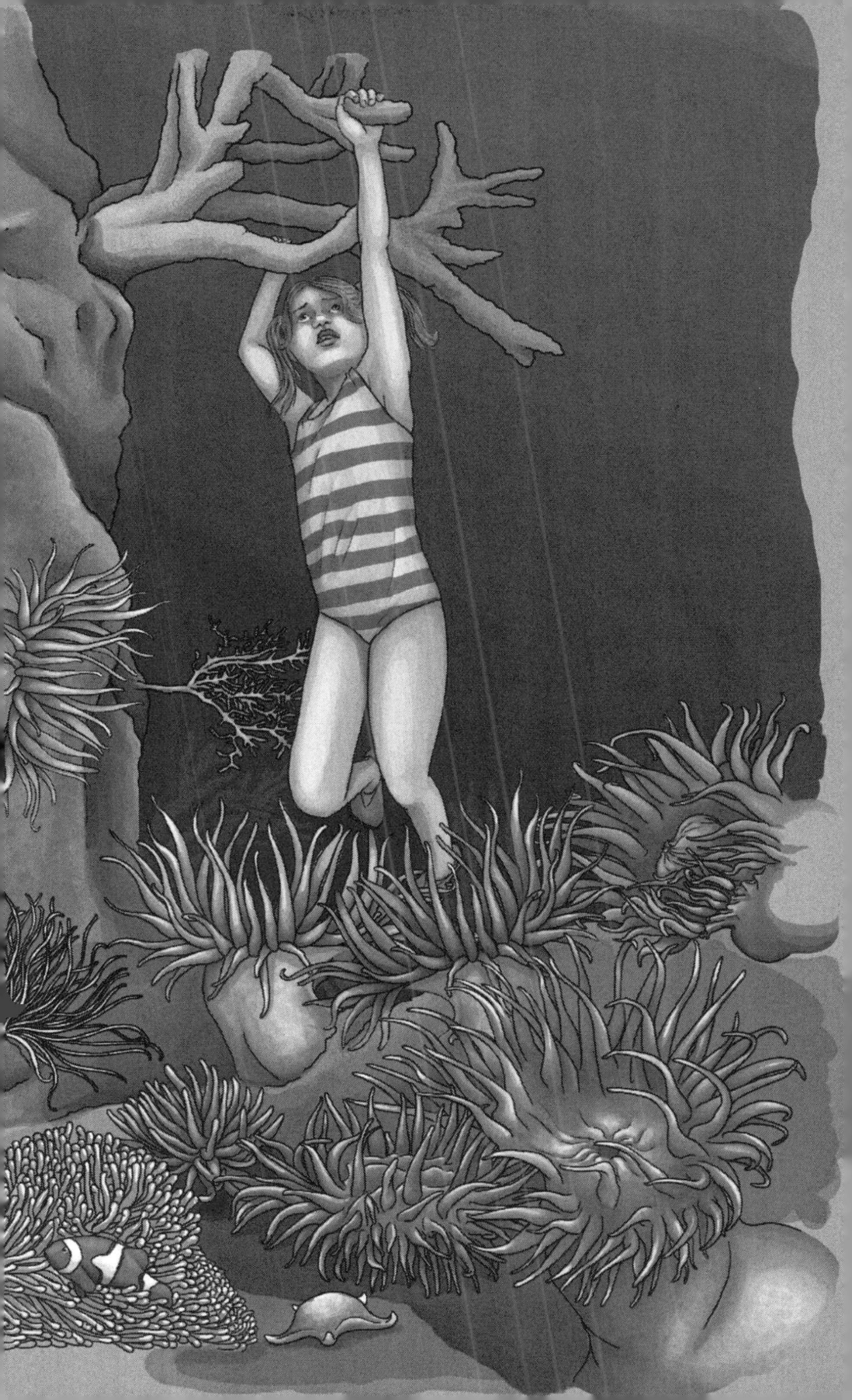

The zebra shark swam so fast and changed directions so quickly that Billy feared they would crash several times. The coral zipped past him in a blur. The shark dodged right to left and left to right, spun around, and even did a complete back flip at one point. It enjoyed the acrobatic maneuvers and showed no sign of slowing.

Billy could see the stripes of the tiger shark to his upper left. It was larger than the zebra shark and was having trouble navigating the dense coral. Soon Billy was directly under the tiger shark and gaining speed. The shark growled at them as it tried to keep up.

Out of nowhere, the hammerhead shark appeared in front of Billy. It had camouflaged itself in the coral and changed its color when Billy was within reach. It thrashed its head at them and they just narrowly missed it.

It then crashed through a branch of coral and swung at the tiger shark. The tiger shark cried as it was hit and it began to fall; its rider, a small girl in pigtails and a white and black striped bathing suit, began to fall with it. She grabbed a piece of coral and held on to it. The tiger shark landed in a nest of coral and got tangled in it. It thrashed about and panicked.

The hammerhead shark and its rider took the opportunity to get out ahead of them.

The bottom and sides of the coral reef were lined with all sorts of sea anemones. They all stirred at the commotion. Billy could see them reaching their tentacles towards the girl and the tiger shark. One had wrapped its tentacle around the girl's swim shoe and started tugging on it as the others stretched towards her. Billy knew from nature documentaries that they were poisonous and would sting and eat fish that swam by.

"We have to help them," he told his shark.

CHAPTER 8

They swam towards the girl and Billy reached out his hand. She grabbed it and he began to pull her onto the back of his shark. The anemone that had her didn't want to let go, but with one final pull she was free minus one swim shoe that the anemone clutched greedily in its tentacle.

The girl said something in a language Billy didn't understand but he assumed it was a thank you so he said, "You're welcome."

Next they reached the tiger shark. It had stopped struggling, but was still very much stuck in the coral. The zebra shark tried to nudge it with its nose. The tiger shark was dazed by the attack but otherwise unhurt. However, the sea anemones were reaching closer to it and Billy knew he had to get it out of there.

He told his shark to lash at the coral with its tail. It did as he instructed and pieces of the coral began to break off. Billy snapped some off as well, careful not to hurt the tiger shark. Eventually the tiger shark was free of the coral, but it wouldn't move.

Billy tried to think of something. He scratched the tiger sharks ears and shook his head but nothing worked. Then he remembered how his friend's cat would always wake up and dart out of the room if you pulled its tail. The shark had a different type of tail but Billy hoped it would still work.

He jumped off the zebra shark and got on top of the tiger shark facing its tail. He reached and started pulling on it. The tiger shark growled loudly and shook Billy as it swam quickly up and away. Billy gripped it tightly; sure he would be tossed off. The girl followed behind on the zebra shark and they carefully navigated the coral until they had swum above it.

Billy turned around on the tiger shark after almost falling off several times and managed to calm it down. Once it regained its composure it purred as Billy scratched its head.

Ahead of them they could see the finish line with a crowd of fish and crustaceans cheering; a cloud of bubbles above their heads. The final

stretch of the race course went over a row of giant clams. They were open, displaying pearls the size of Billy! They looked tempting, but Billy knew the clam would snap shut if he got too close.

The tiger shark and zebra shark swam side by side the rest of the way. Billy and the girl swam towards the finish line and they could see that four sharks had already crossed. "Looks like we lost," he said.

Michelle on the ghost shark managed to sneak ahead of everyone and win. The hammerhead and

its pug-nosed, mean-faced rider won second place, and the leopard shark was third. The bull shark managed to get free but wasn't able to place.

Billy and the girl crossed the finish line in fifth and sixth place respectively. He watched as the puffer fish placed a golden shell around Michelle's neck. The crowd applauded and cheered, though Billy couldn't hear any of it, he could only see the bubbles their mouths made. The silver shell went to the mean boy, and the bronze shell went to the girl in the red bathing suit.

The Jellyfish Monster that had brought Billy to the underwater city swam over and patted Billy on the head.

"I'm sorry I didn't win," he said.

The Jellyfish Monster only shrugged.

CHAPTER 9

A big parade started in the underwater city. Crustaceans started drumming on scallop shells. A narwhal began to whistle using its long horn like a flute. Several whales sang in high pitch echoes. The crowd let go of their bubble-balloons and they floated happily above them, caught in the current. Sea horses galloped gleefully around the streets of the city.

All sorts of strange fish followed and danced behind the processions. There were fish that had fins bigger than their bodies that reminded Billy of butterflies. There were see-through blobs twisting around and fish that would change shape every time they breathed. Shell-covered crustaceans with hundreds of tiny feet frolicked about. There were furry animals with duck bills and long tails, and mollusks darting around, hidden inside their shells of all shapes and colors.

There were bright colored fish and fish that blended into the environment. There were some with stripes and spots and some with patterns that changed as they swam. It seemed like the entire city was out and bustling around. Billy didn't recognize half the sea creatures, and suspected no one else would believe they existed.

Five mermen rode on top of stingrays as if they were surfboards. They swam in formation doing spectacular flips and maneuvers. Everyone applauded and cheered as they passed over their heads.

"Isn't it amazing?" Michelle asked. She had swum over to Billy and the girl with pigtails. Billy agreed and they watched the celebration together.

Off to the side, Billy noticed the Jellyfish Monster that brought the bully to the race went over to the boy. The monster was dark red with black swirls. It had three spiral horns on top of its head and spikes on its fins.

It put its tentacles on its hips and started spouting bubbles at the kid. Even without understanding what it was saying, it was clear that it was mad. The tentacles under its head trembled. The scene was extremely intimidating.

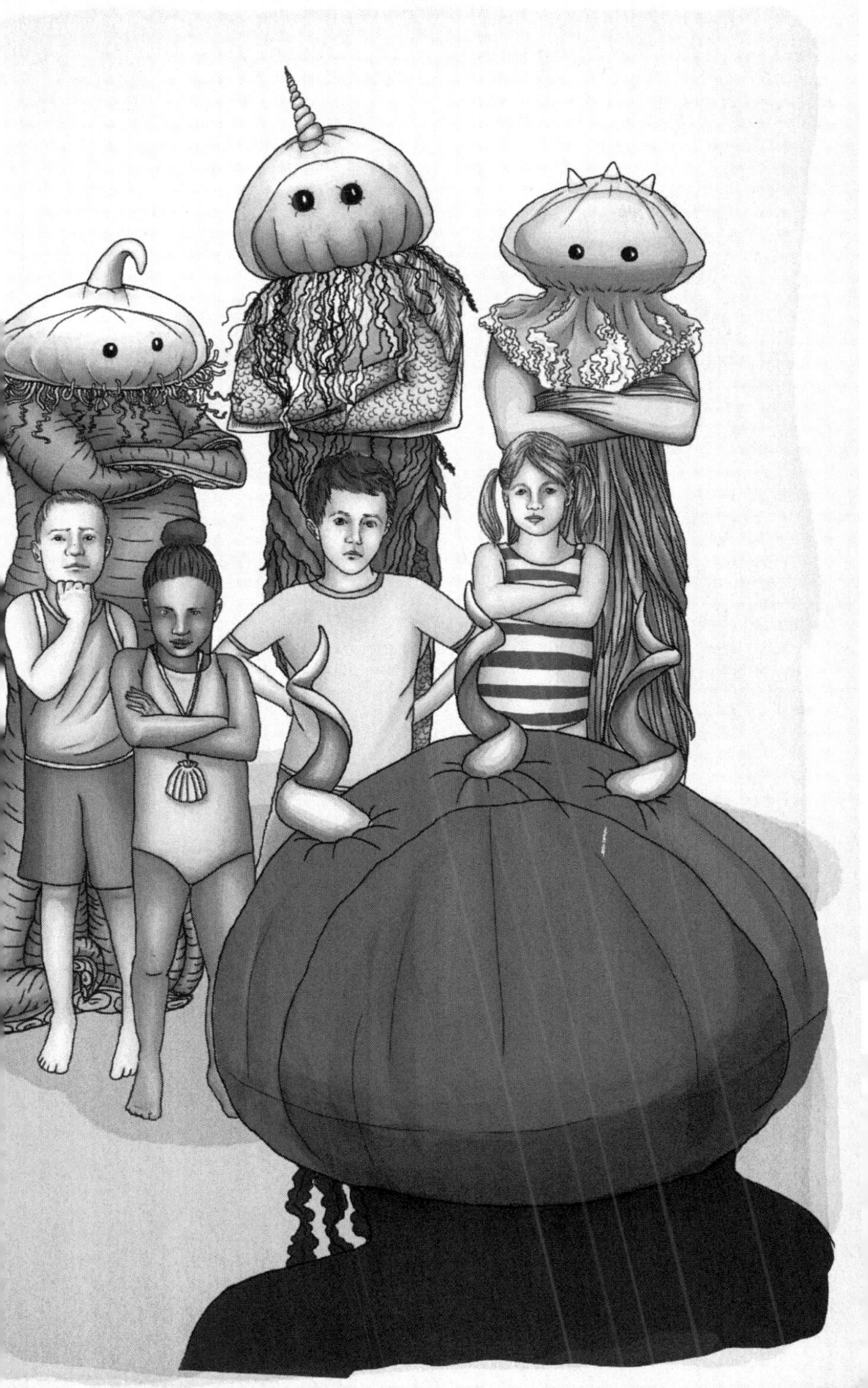

The boy flinched and backed away. His eyes were wide as they stared at the furious monster. The monster reached forward and yanked the silver medal away from his neck. It then pushed the boy.

Billy, Michelle, and the girl with pigtails swam over and stood between the bully and the red Jellyfish Monster. They crossed their arms and scowled at the creature. It looked surprised at first and then even angrier than it had before. Finally the three Jellyfish Monsters that accompanied Billy, Michelle, and the girl came over.

Michelle's monster was short and pudgy with two tentacles for hands and four for feet. Round suckers lined the inside of each tentacle. Its head was wide and flat with a single curled horn on top. Thin, stringy tentacles hung under its head, floating about like spaghetti.

The foreign girl's monster was taller and thin. It had three short, stubby horns on top of its head. Its hands and feet were long, flat flippers. Under its head, wide, wavy flaps draped over its chest and shoulders. It looked almost like a skirt, or blanket.

It wore long, straight strands of seaweed that were wrapped neatly over its body.

Seeing that he was severely outnumbered, the red Jellyfish Monster swam away and left them alone.

The mean boy frowned at the group that saved him. After what he did to Billy and the girl, he couldn't understand why they helped him.

After a moment, he whispered, "Thanks." He kept his head tilted down, not wanting to look them in the eye. "I'm sorry," he added.

"It's okay," Billy replied. "Just be more careful next time."

"Why did you do it?" Michelle asked him.

"I didn't want to lose," the boy admitted. "My mom and dad get upset when I lose."

"Sometimes you lose," Michelle told him. "It's okay."

"You can't hurt other people to win," Billy added. "That's not nice."

"Okay," he said.

The girl nodded and said something in a language none of them knew.

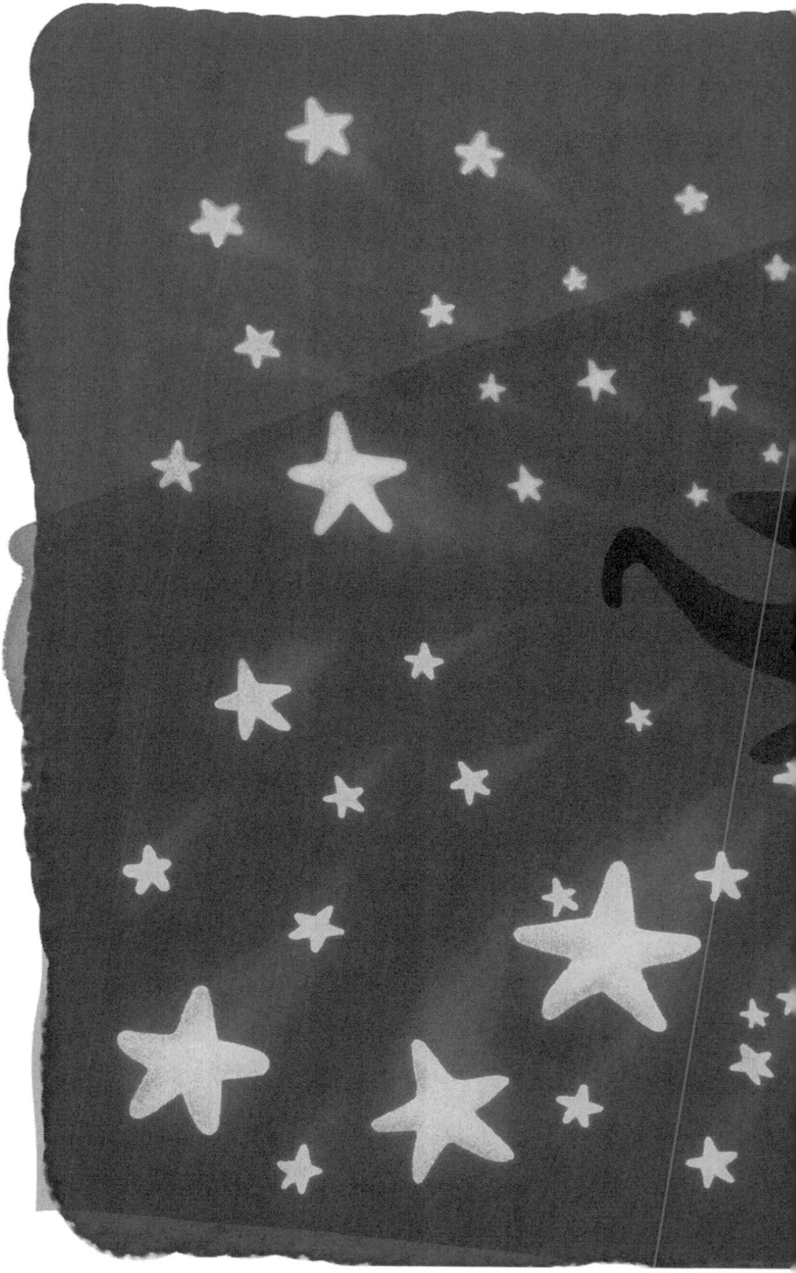

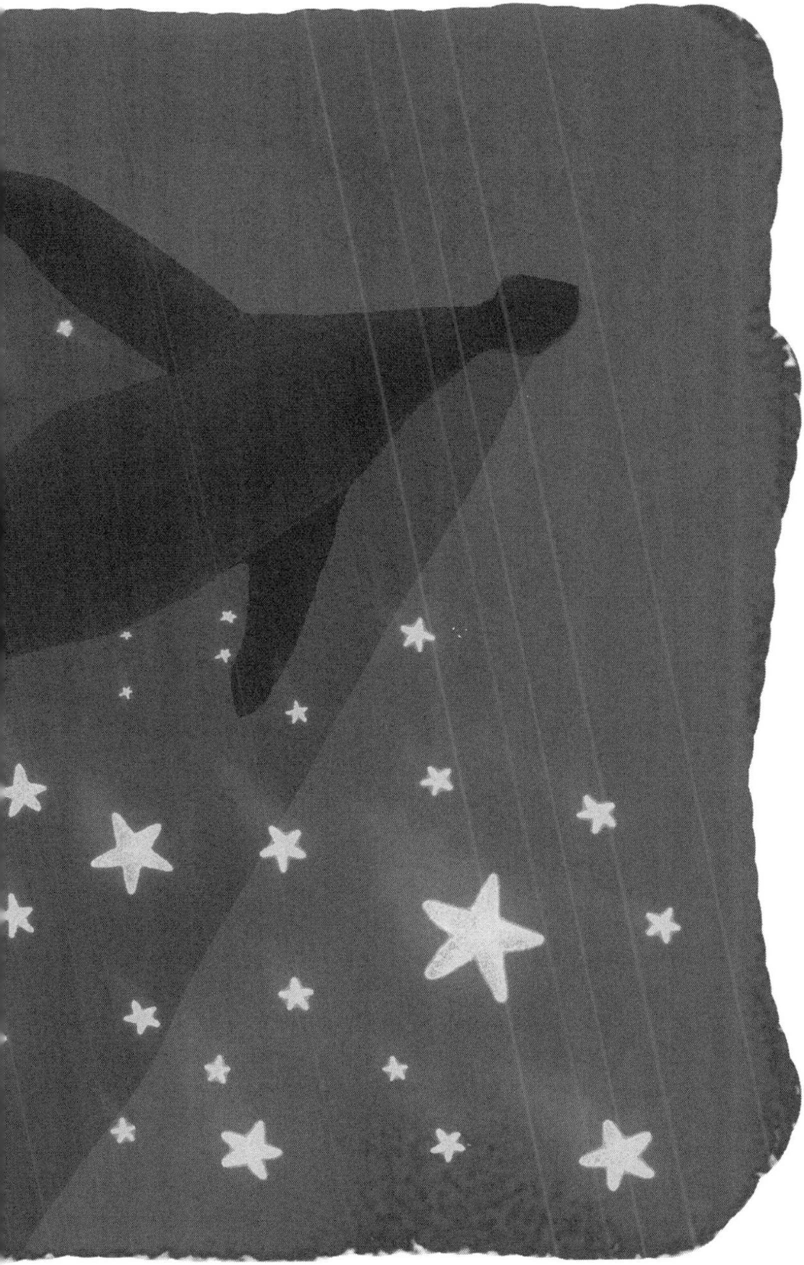

"What's your name?" Michelle asked the boy.

"Tommy," he replied.

"Come on, Tommy, let's watch the rest of the parade," Michelle said smiling.

They joined the rest of the racers who had finally made their way back and watched the festivities. It was hard to tell how long it went on; there were no underwater clocks. Billy's father had a waterproof watch. *I'll have to borrow it next time*, he thought to himself.

For the finale, a large dinosaur that looked like the Loch Ness Monster swam above the city and dropped thousands of tiny, glowing starfish. They streaked down towards the crowd like falling stars. Each one changed colors at it fell - from blue to green to purple to orange to yellow to red to pink and back to blue.

CHAPTER 10

Eventually, the crowd began to thin and the children were once again fully inside giant bubbles floating back to wherever they came from. Billy and the Jellyfish Monster floated above the park and a large sea turtle drifted lazily over to them. They landed on its back and were carried away on its massive shell.

In the distance Billy saw a school of dolphins swim by. A few of them did somersaults in the water, playfully showing off. He waved to them and it almost looked like they waved back.

"Will there be another race?" Billy asked.

The Jellyfish Monster nodded.

"When?"

The monster shrugged.

The turtle swam past a giant squid perched on top of a sunken oil tanker. It clung to it protectively as they passed by. Its single eye was as large as Billy was and it glared at the travelers for as long as they could tell.

Billy kept looking over his shoulder to make sure the giant squid wasn't following them.

As they passed through a tall forest of kelp, a school of flat, circular fish approached the turtle to investigate Billy and the Jellyfish Monster. Their bodies were covered in gold and silver scales that Billy could see his reflection in. His image stretched as the fish moved, like a fun house mirror.

"Maybe you can come visit me sometime," Billy suggested.

The Jellyfish Monster's tentacles flailed upward excitedly.

Billy laughed. "We have races at school on field day. I guess it'd be boring compared to all this."

The monster shook his head no. Billy smiled.

Several penguins swished by chasing blue fish. They had yellow hair on their heads that made them look like they had big, bushy eyebrows. One swam over to Billy and tried to offer the fish to him.

"No, thank you," Billy declined politely.

The fish fled when the penguin opened its beak. The bird then spun around and chased after it.

At one point Billy was quite surprised when a large sea dragon passed overhead. He gazed upward at the green scales of the dragon. Its long body slithered by for a full minute before the tail passed and the dragon disappeared into the distance.

"No one is going to believe any of this," Billy said in amazement.

The Jellyfish Monster looked around and then scratched its head.

The sunlight above them grew brighter and brighter, blinding Billy who had grown accustomed to the darkness of the ocean. Soon he found himself on the beach standing in front of the hole he was digging when he first discovered the Jellyfish Monster.

He looked around and could see his brothers still in the water. No one else noticed the giant creature standing in front of him.

"I guess you're going back now, huh?"

The Jellyfish Monster nodded.

"I had fun, thanks for taking me."

The Jellyfish Monster reached out and placed

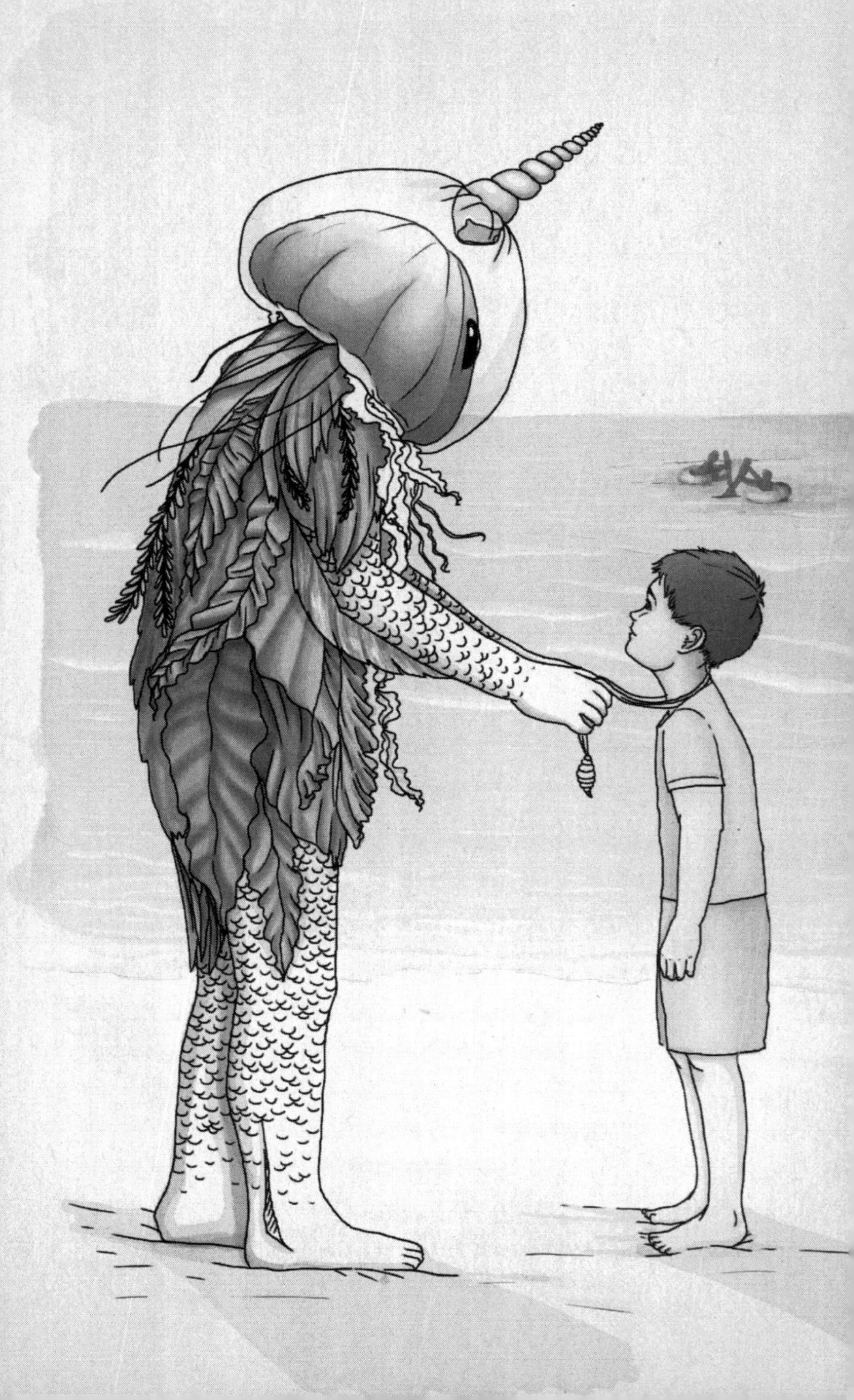

something around Billy's neck. It was the silver medal - a silver shell with specks of blue and green glinting off the sunlight.

Billy held it in his hands and cocked his head to the side. "How did you get this?"

The monster shrugged.

"Did you steal it from the mean monster?"

It nodded.

"But I didn't win."

The Jellyfish Monster nodded and sank into the wet sand.

Billy stood at the shallow hole he had dug and reached inside. It was empty. He looked down at the shell around his neck and smiled.

"Whatcha got there, Billy?" his father asked returning from his walk.

"A prize. I won second place, though I didn't really. I was cheated out of it, but I got the prize anyway."

"Find it digging, huh? Never know what's buried out here. Let me know if you find any gold or cash," his father chuckled.

"Okay," Billy said.

"Your mom went back to the hotel for lunch, you hungry yet?" his dad asked.

Billy nodded.

"All right, let me get your brothers and we'll go get some sandwiches or something," Billy's dad said.

"Okay," he said.

His dad then went into the ocean, hopping over the waves, trying to get his sons' attention. A large wave came and knocked him down onto his butt. He stood back up and made it over to his sons.

Billy, his father, and his two brothers tip toed back over the hot sand and then over the hot pavement until they got to the Pink Flamingo, the motel where they were staying. They climbed the steps to room 302 and walked into the almost too cold, air-conditioned room. There were sandwiches and chips on the table waiting for them.

Billy scarfed down his lunch as quickly as he could. He didn't realize just how hungry he was (shark racing can work up quite the appetite).

"Slow down, it's not a race," his mother warned.

He studied the shell as he waited anxiously for

the rest of his family to finish so he could go back to the beach. He wondered what he would discover next.

About the Author

Bryan Kwasnik grew up in Jefferson Township, NJ. He has been scribbling stories about all sorts of strange things since he was a child. He also writes and records music. He currently resides in Belleville, NJ with his girlfriend, Bridgette. This is his first early chapter book.